THE LAZIEST ROBOT IN ZONE ONE

Lillian & Phoebe Hoban

THE
LAZIEST ROBOT
IN ZONE ONE

Pictures by Lillian Hoban

Harper & Row, Publishers

An I CAN READ Book

45274

The Laziest Robot in Zone One
Copyright © 1983 by Lillian Hoban and Phoebe Hoban
All rights reserved. No part of this book may be
used or reproduced in any manner whatsoever without
written permission except in the case of brief quotations
embodied in critical articles and reviews. Printed in
the United States of America. For information address
Harper & Row, Publishers, Inc., 10 East 53rd Street,
New York, N.Y. 10022: Published simultaneously in
Canada by Fitzhenry & Whiteside Limited, Toronto.
1 2 3 4 5 6 7 8 9 10
First Edition

Library of Congress Cataloging in Publication Data
Hoban, Lillian.
    The laziest robot in zone one.

    (An I can read book)
    Summary: Sol-l helps all his friends with their
work in the process of avoiding his own.
    [1. Robots—Fiction.   2. Helpfulness—Fiction.
3. Work—Fiction]   I. Hoban, Phoebe.   II. Title.
III. Series.
PZ7.H635Laz 1983   [E]   82-48613
ISBN 0-06-022349-9
ISBN 0-06-022352-9 (lib. bdg.)

For Esmé

It was Game Time.

Sola was playing

with her Uni-Doll.

Sol-1 was watching a holo-disc.

"My Uni-Doll is broken,"

said Sola.

"Will you help me fix it?"

"Later," said Sol-1.

"I am watching the Laser Tones.

They are my favorite group."

He turned up the sound

very loud.

"Stop all that noise,"

said Mama-Sol.

"Game Time is over."

"I just want to finish

watching this disc,"

said Sol-1.

"But you have not done your homework,
or weeded the space garden,
or walked the dog," said Mama-Sol.
"He hasn't fixed my Uni-Doll
either," said Sola.

"Sometimes I think you are
the laziest robot in Zone One,"
said Mama-Sol.
"Now turn off that disc and
take Big Rover for a walk."

"Work, work, and more work,"

said Sol-1.

And he rolled outside.

"I will come too," said Sola.

"We can play Space Tag

with Big Rover."

11

But Big Rover was not

in his dog dock.

Sol-1 blinked his lights.

"I guess I forgot to lock it,"

he said.

"Rover, Rover," he called.

But Big Rover did not come.

"Big Rover is lost!" said Sola.

"We better find him

before Down Time!"

"We better find him

before Mama-Sol finds out,"

said Sol-1.

They looked under the Super-Track

and on top of the sun shield.

They looked in the space garden

and behind the disc disposal.

But they didn't find Big Rover.

"This is hard work," said Sol-1.

"I don't like work.

There has to be a better way

to find him."

Sol-1's controls started humming.

Suddenly,

all of his lights flashed.

His control panel lit up.

"I've got it!" he said.

"We can invite the other robots

to a search party

for Big Rover!

Then it won't be like work!"

"You are a pretty smart robot,"

said Sola.

Sol-1 and Sola rolled

to Super Scan's house first.

Super Scan was in his space garden.

"Big Rover is lost,

and we are having a search party,"

called Sol-1. "Want to come?"

"Not now," yelled Super Scan.
"I have to weed the space garden,
and I can't catch all the weeds."
Giant purple and red puff weeds
were drifting
all around the space garden.

19

Super Scan tried to catch a red one.

It exploded into hundreds

of little puff weeds.

Then he tried to catch a purple one.

But that exploded too.

"You should catch weeds
before they get too big,"
called Sola.

"I know," yelled Super Scan.
"You will have to have
the search party without me."
Sol-1 blinked his lights.
"I will help you," he said.

Sol-1 took Super Scan's weed catcher.

He waved it in front of him

and rolled around the space garden.

All the puff weeds swirled

around and around very fast.

They made a giant puff-weed cloud.

Then Sol-1 waved the weed catcher

in front of the cloud.

The cloud whirled toward the corner

of the garden.

"Quick, open the weed disposal,"

yelled Sol-1 to Super Scan.

"I will shoo all the weeds right in."

Super Scan opened the weed disposal.

The giant puff-weed cloud

began to disappear into it.

"Sol-1 sure knows how to catch

big puff weeds," said Super Scan.

"That's because he always lets

the weeds in our garden

get too big," said Sola.

24

Suddenly, a giant puff weed

left the cloud.

It zoomed straight at Sol-1.

"Look out!" yelled Super Scan.

"If it hits you it will explode.

You will have to start all over!"

Sol-1 ducked just as the puff weed

was about to hit him.

Quickly, he spun around

and held up the weed catcher.

The puff weed flew straight in.

Sol-1 rolled to the weed disposal.

He threw in the puff weed.

"Great! My garden is all weeded,"

said Super Scan.

"Now we can go

on the search party!"

"Party!" said Rocko.

He rolled up behind them.

"Did you say party?"

Rocko's built-in jukebox lit up.

"It's a search party for Big Rover,"
said Sola.

"We're going to invite
Micromax and Fax and Arla...."

"I'll come too," said Rocko.

"You can't have a party
without music."

Rocko played a little song

as they rolled to Micromax's house:

"*Big Rover, Big Rover,*

It's time to come home.

It soon will be Down Time—

It's no time to roam."

But Big Rover did not come.

Micromax was swimming

in the solar pond

in front of his house.

"We're having a search party,"

called Sol-1.

"Do you want to come?"

"I can't," yelled Micromax.

"I'm doing my homework.

I have to find out how hot it is

at the bottom of the solar pond,

and I can't dive down there."

"Let me try," said Sol-1.

Sol-1 dove into the water.

But he bobbed straight up

like a cork.

He flew into the air

and splashed down again.

This time he floated on the water.

His lights blinked on and off.

His controls spluttered.

"I am not heavy enough,"

said Sol-1.

"The salt that stores the heat

is making me float."

"I'll get a weight," said Sola.

"And I'll get some rope

and tie it to you," said Micromax.

Sola got a weight,

and Micromax tied it to Sol-1.

Sol-1 dived back into the solar pond.

This time he sank like a stone.

It was very hot on the bottom.

It was so hot that Sol-1's alarms

started to bleep.

• DANGER ALERT: BURN OUT •

flashed his control panel.

His temperature shot up to 1000°.

"Wow! Now I know how hot it is
on the bottom," said Sol-1.
"I better swim up
before my controls melt."
Sol-1 tried to untie the weight
so he could swim up.
But the harder he pulled,
the tighter the knot became.

Sol-1 started to get scared.

He could hear the other robots

calling to him above the water.

"Why didn't I look for Big Rover
by myself?" he thought.
"Then I wouldn't be in hot water.
If only I could slip the rope
over my head."
Sol-1 blinked his lights.

"Slip," he said.

"It's a slipknot, and

I've been pulling the wrong way!"

Quickly, Sol-1 pulled

the end of the rope.

The knot slipped out,

and the weight fell down.

Sol-1 shot straight up
out of the water.

His lights blinked on and off.

"I'll tell you how hot it is

on the bottom," he said to Micromax.

"It is very, *very* hot!

It is over 1000°!"

"Good," said Micromax.

"You finished all of my homework."

"Now let's get Arla and Fax,

and go on the search party,"

said Sola.

Rocko played a song as they rolled

to Fax and Arla's house:

"Big Rover, Big Rover,

Where are you now?

We're looking all over—

Why don't you bow-wow!"

But Big Rover did not answer.

Fax and Arla were

in back of their house.

They were looking up

at the wind power station.

"We're going on a search party,"

called Sol-1. "Want to come?"

"Sshh!" said Arla.

"Don't make any noise!"

"Why not?" asked Micromax.

Fax pointed to the top

of the wind station.

All the robots looked up.

The windmill was spinning

very slowly.

On one of its blades

was a tiny black dot.

"What is it?" asked Sola.

"Our cat, Power Puss,"

answered Arla.

"She is afraid to come down."

"We think some dog

chased her up there," said Fax.

"You better get her before Down Time,"
said Super Scan.

"You better get her down
before that dog comes back,"
said Micromax.

"I hope it was not Big Rover!"
Sola whispered to Sol-1.

Sol-1 blinked his lights.

"I bet it *was* Big Rover,"

he whispered to Sola.

"Well, what goes up

must come down," he said.

And he climbed up the ladder

on the side of the windmill.

Sol-1 grabbed
one windmill blade.
He hooked on
to another blade
with his wheels.

Then he hung upside down

and reached for Power Puss.

Suddenly there was a howling noise.

The windmill started to shake.

The windmill shook so hard

that it rattled.

"Hurry!" called Sola.

"The windmill is making

a funny noise!

Something is wrong

with the controls!"

Sol-1 tried to grab Power Puss.

But she arched her back and hissed.

The windmill swayed back and forth.

There was a loud swooshing sound.

Sol-1 looked down.

Something was coming

out of the control dock!

It was wagging its tail!

It was Big Rover!

Big Rover shook himself all over
and stretched.

Then he opened his mouth very wide
and yawned.

Power Puss looked down.

When she saw Big Rover,

she jumped straight

into Sol-1's arms.

"Bow wow wow!" barked Big Rover.

"Hold Big Rover," called Sol-1.

"I'm coming down!"

He held Power Puss tight

and jumped.

"*Bleep! Bleep!*" cheered the robots.

"*BOW WOW WOW!*"

barked Big Rover.

"*Hiiissss,*" said Power Puss.

Arla hugged Power Puss.

"Now we can go

on a search party," she said.

"But we already found
what we were searching for,"
said Sola.

"Let's have a party anyway,"
said Sol-1.

"It's time for some fun
after all that hard work."

"You did work hard," said Sola.
"Maybe you are not
the laziest robot in Zone One."

"That is not what Mama-Sol will say," said Sol-1. "Wait till she finds out I have not done my homework or weeded the space garden."

"That's right," said Sola.

"And it is almost Down Time!"

Sol-1 blinked his lights.

All the robots looked at him.

"Don't worry," said Super Scan.

"You helped us, now we will help you."

"Let's go!" shouted the robots.

"Let's all go help Sol-1!"

They all rolled to Sol-1's house.

"It is almost Down Time,"

said Mama-Sol.

"You took Rover for a long walk.

Did you finish your homework?"

"I am going to do that now,"

said Sol-1.

"My friends will weed the garden."

"Yes," said Super Scan.

"Sol-1 helped *me* weed *my* garden."

"And he helped me finish my

homework," said Micromax.

"And he helped us save our cat,"

said Arla and Fax.

"That doesn't sound like
my lazy little robot," said Mama-Sol.
"That sounds like a very hard worker."
She hugged Sol-1.
"It is nice when robots
work together," Mama-Sol said.

Rocko played on his jukebox:

"When robots work together

Things get done 1, 2, 3.

Hurry up robots!

Roll along with me.

We will finish all the work,

And there will still be time for fun.

HURRY UP, ROBOTS!

COME ON, EVERYONE!"

So all the robots helped Sol-1.

And when they were finished,

they danced until Down Time.